BILLY TARTLE
IN
SAY
CHEESE!

BY
MICHAEL
TOWNSEND

Alfred A. Knopf
new york

WHAT'S GOOEY, JUICY, STICKY, AND FUN?

WHY, GOOEY, JUICY, STICKY FUN POPS, of course

THEY'RE Fun-tastic

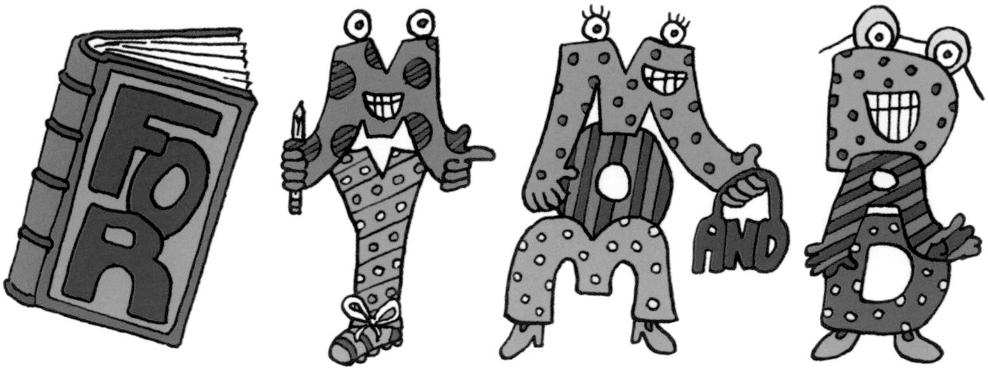
FOR
AND

THIS IS A BORZOI BOOK PUBLISHED BY ALFRED A. KNOPF

Published in the United States by Alfred A. Knopf, an imprint of Random House Children's Books, a division of Random House, Inc., New York.

KNOPF, BORZOI BOOKS, and the colophon are registered trademarks of Random House, Inc.

www.randomhouse.com/kids

Educators and librarians, for a variety of teaching tools, visit us at www.randomhouse.com/teachers

Library of Congress Cataloging-in-Publication Data
Townsend, Michael (Michael Jay).
Billy Tartle in Say cheese! / written and illustrated by Michael Townsend.
p. cm.
SUMMARY: Billy is determined to find a way to make his school picture much more memorable.
ISBN 978-0-375-83932-0 (trade) — ISBN 978-0-375-93932-7 (lib. bdg.)
[1. Photographs—Fiction. 2. Schools—Fiction.] I. Title.
PZ7.T6639Bil 2007
[E]—dc22
2006024354

The illustrations in this book were created using black pen and ink and digital coloring.

MANUFACTURED IN CHINA
July 2007
10 9 8 7 6 5 4 3 2 1
First Edition

1 DAY BEFORE PICTURE DAY

SQUEAK-A
SQUEAK-A
SQUEAK-A
WHAT WAS THAT, PROFESSOR CHEW TOY?
SQUEAK-A
SQUEAK-A
YOU'RE SOOO RIGHT! IF I DON'T GET GOING I'll MISS SUPERMONKEY
GOODBYE, PUDDLES!
SLURP

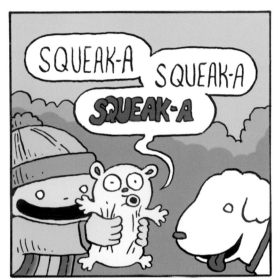

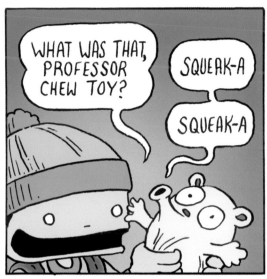

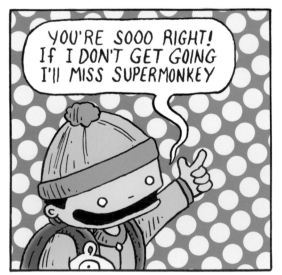

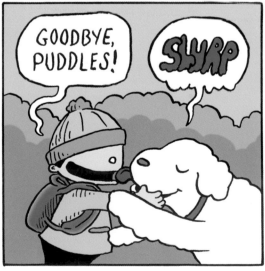

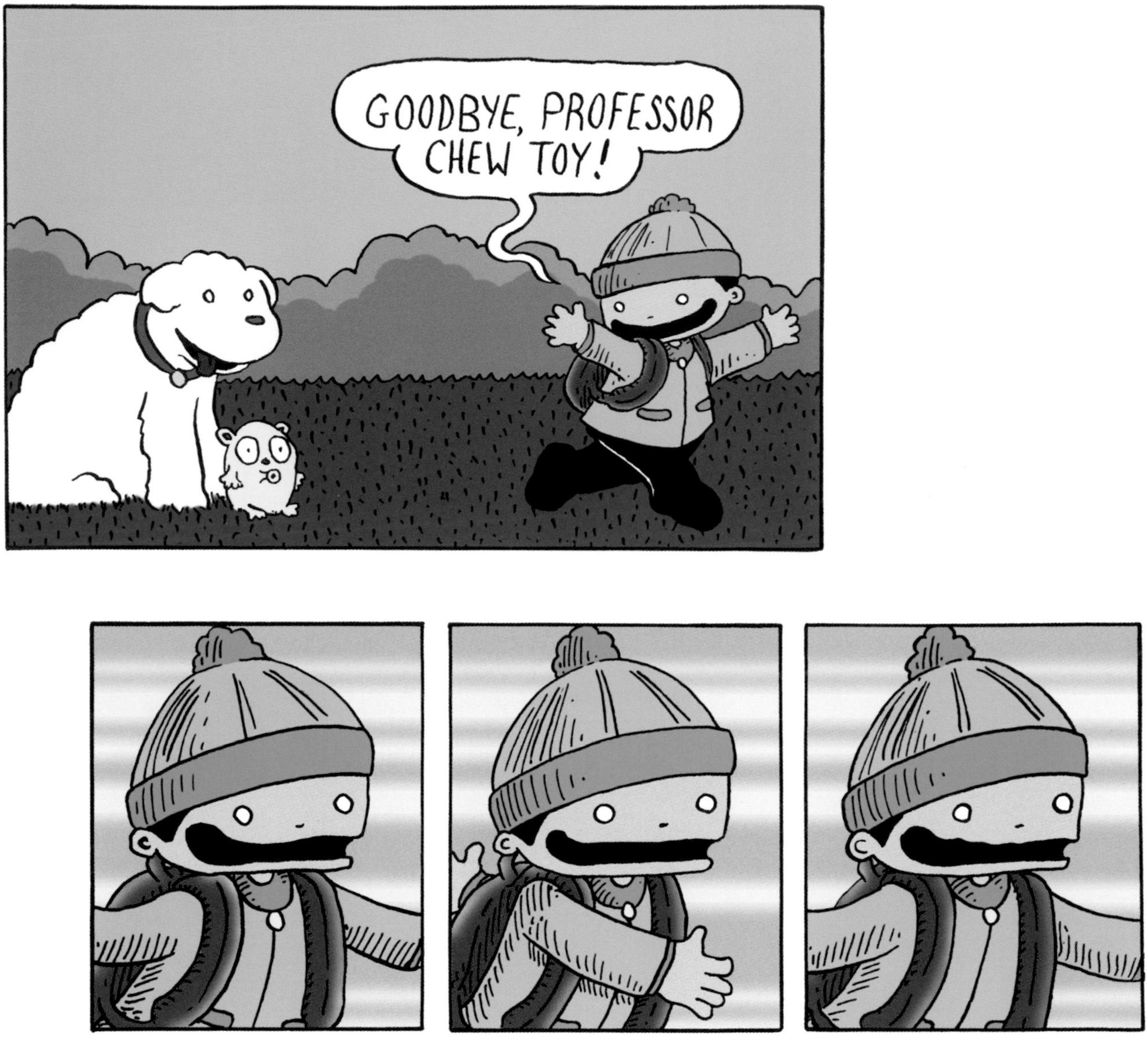
GOODBYE, PROFESSOR CHEW TOY!

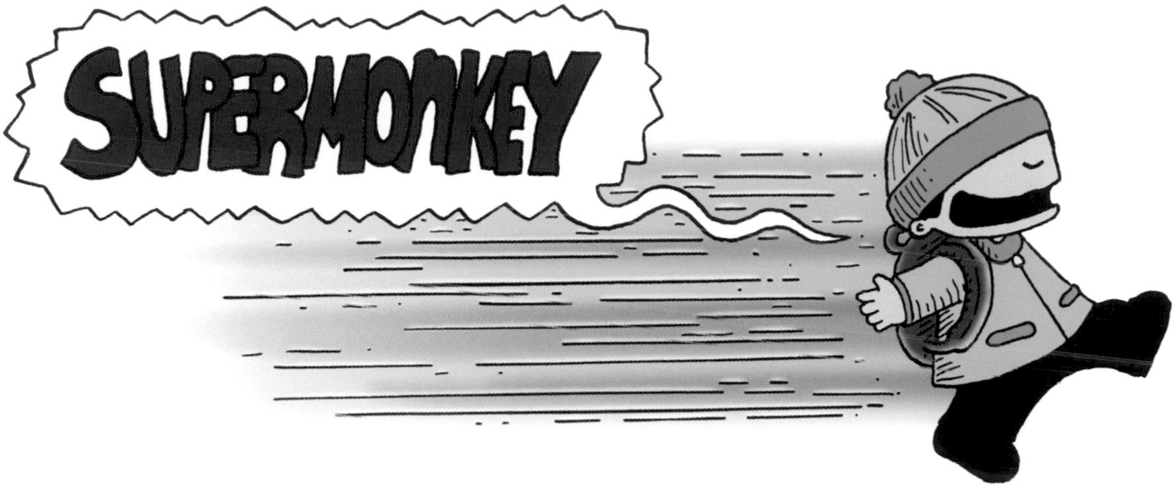
SUPERMONKEY

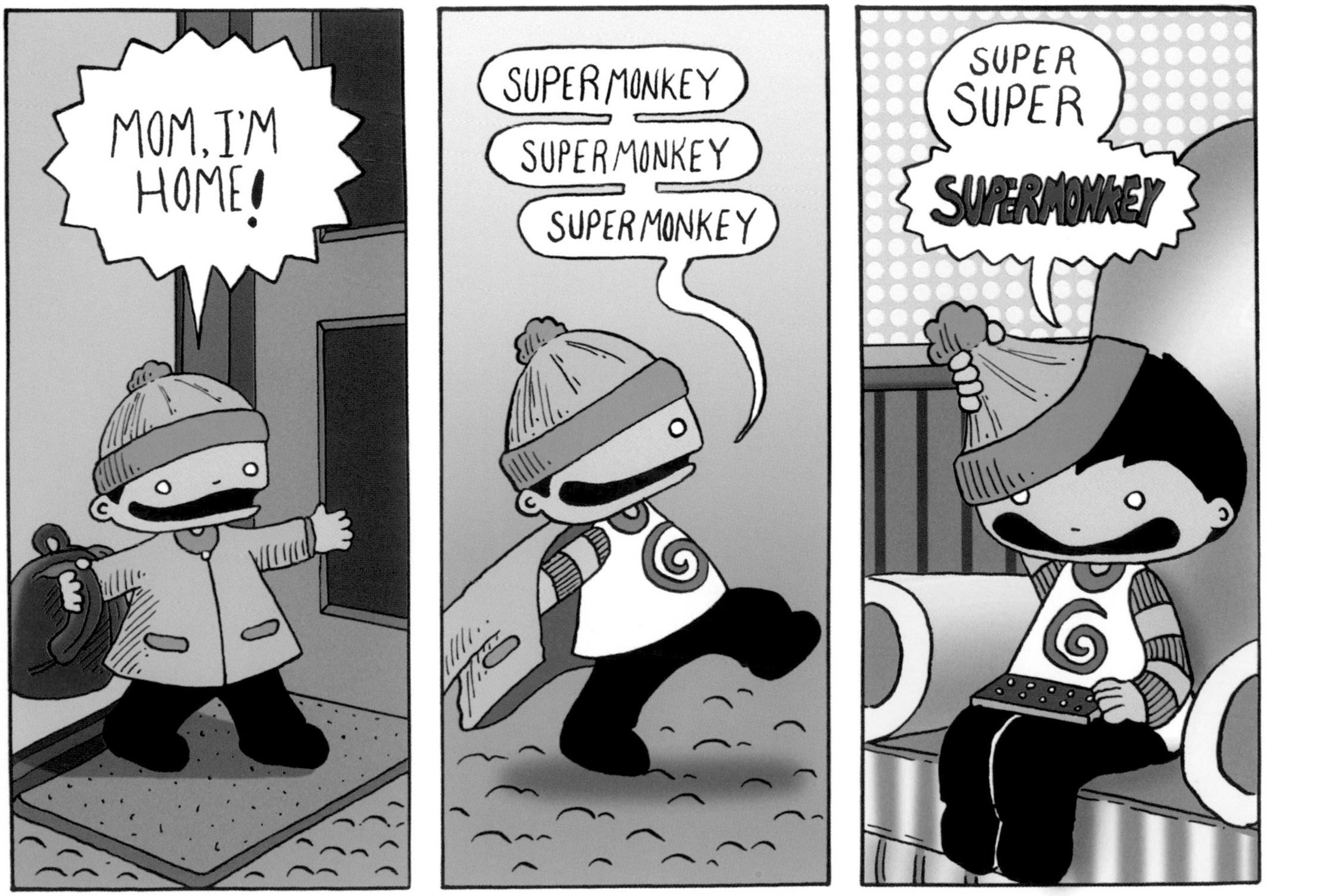
MOM, I'M HOME!
SUPER MONKEY
SUPER MONKEY
SUPER MONKEY
SUPER SUPER
SUPERMONKEY

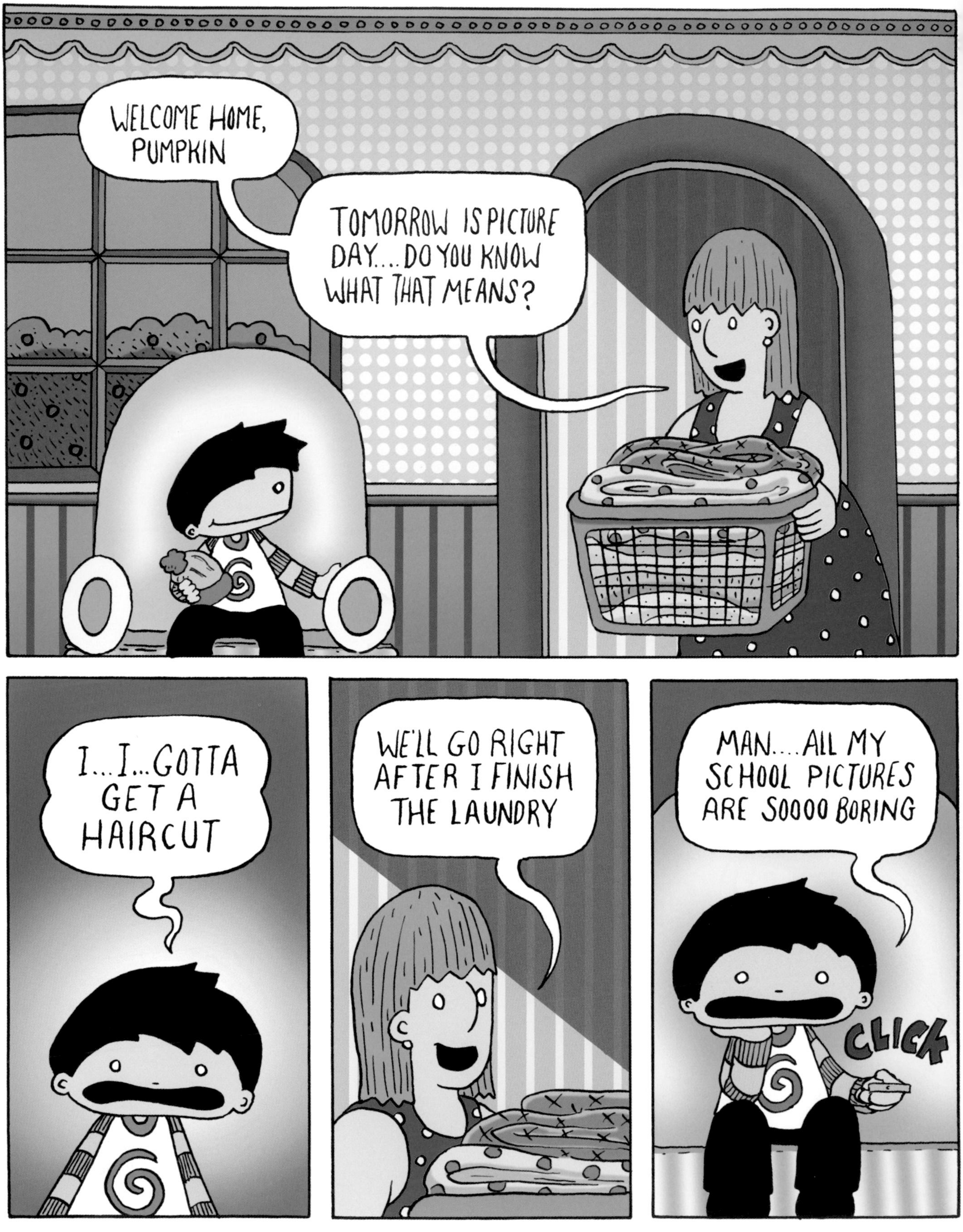
WELCOME HOME, PUMPKIN
TOMORROW IS PICTURE DAY.... DO YOU KNOW WHAT THAT MEANS?
I...I...GOTTA GET A HAIRCUT
WE'LL GO RIGHT AFTER I FINISH THE LAUNDRY
MAN.... ALL MY SCHOOL PICTURES ARE SOOOO BORING
CLICK

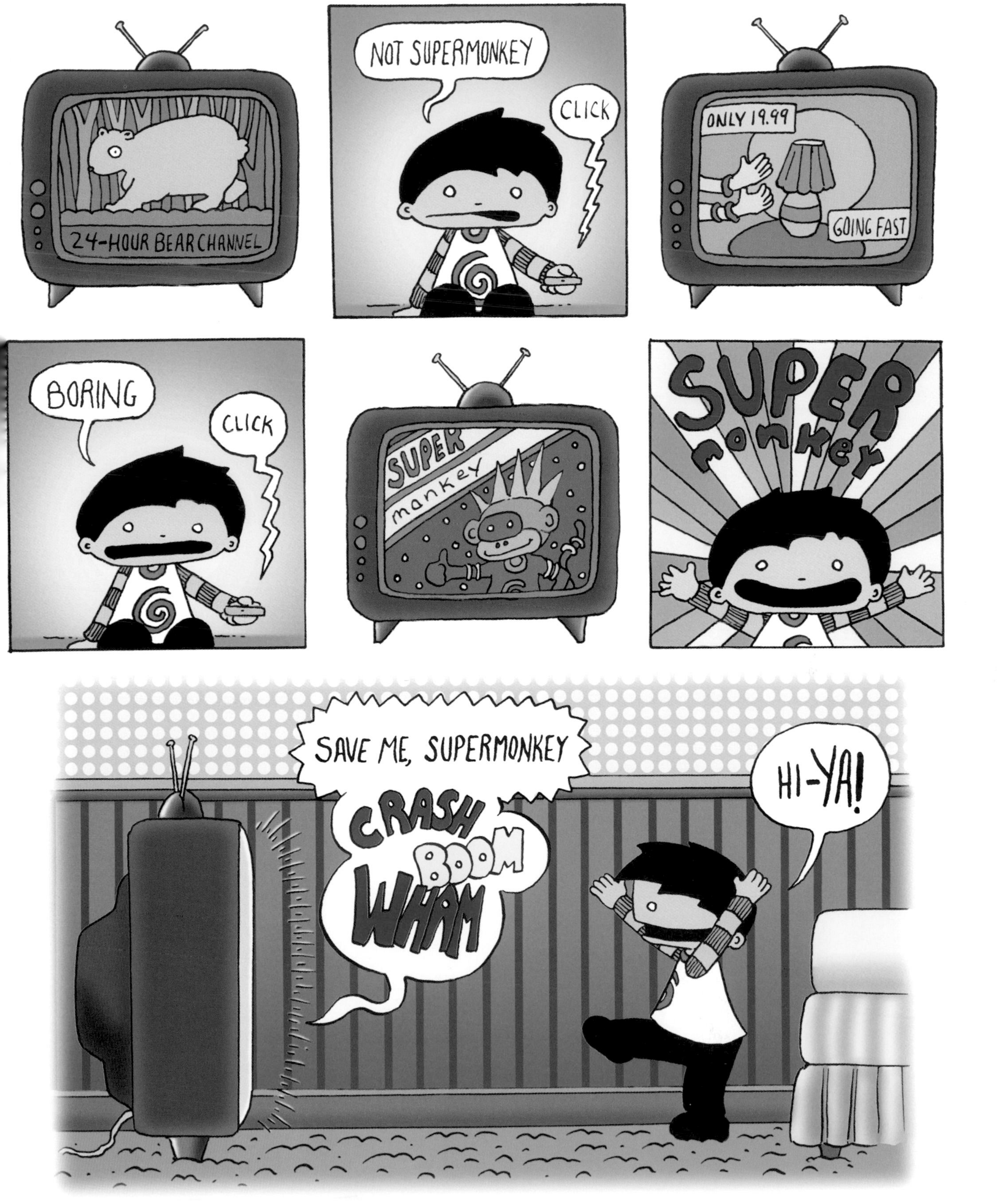
24-HOUR BEAR CHANNEL
NOT SUPERMONKEY
CLICK
ONLY 19.99
GOING FAST
BORING
CLICK
SUPER monkey
SUPER monkey
SAVE ME, SUPERMONKEY
CRASH BOOM WHAM
HI-YA!

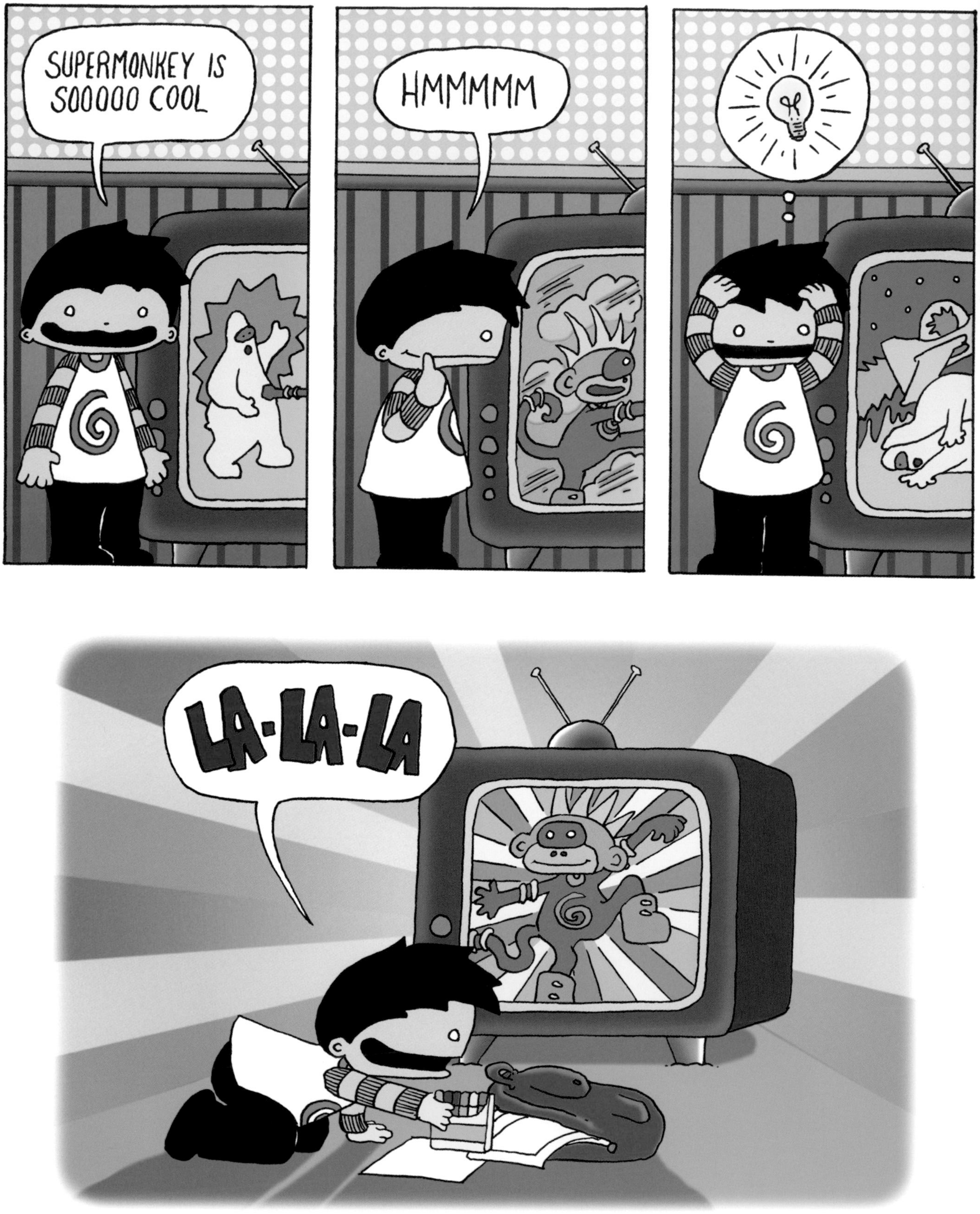
SUPERMONKEY IS SOOOOO COOL
HMMMMM
LA-LA-LA

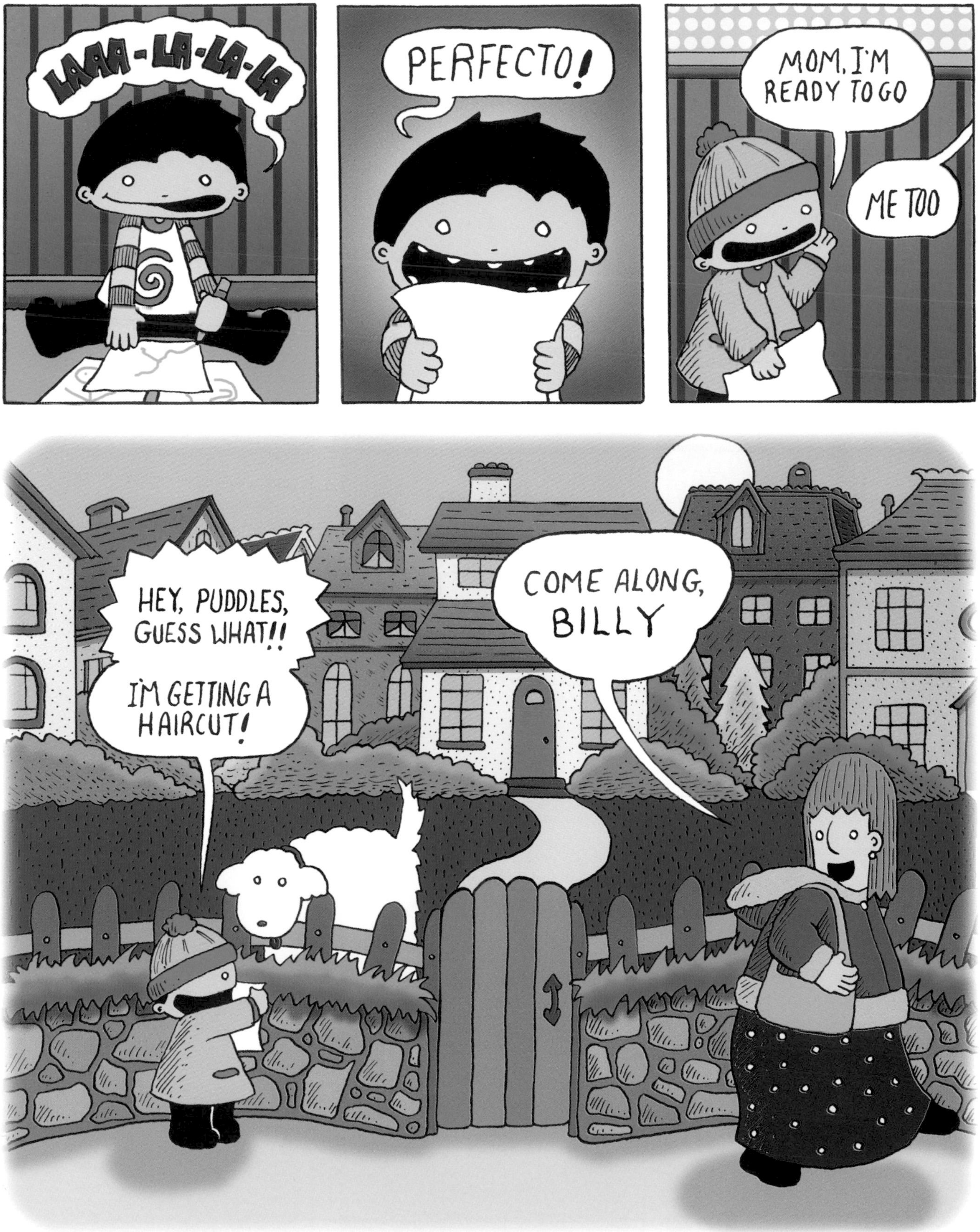
LAAA-LA-LA-LA
PERFECTO!
MOM, I'M READY TO GO
ME TOO
HEY, PUDDLES, GUESS WHAT!!
I'M GETTING A HAIRCUT!
COME ALONG, BILLY

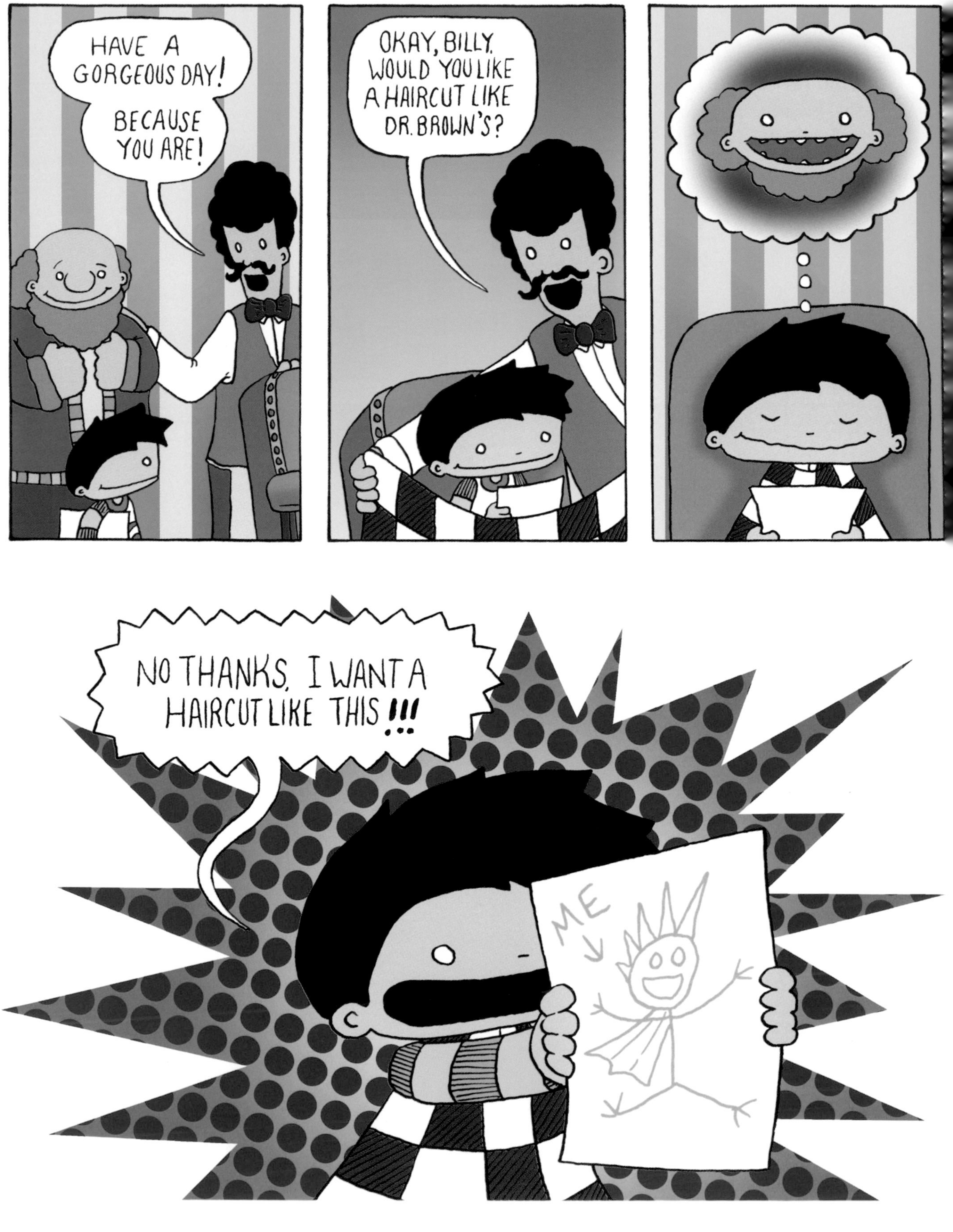
HAVE A GORGEOUS DAY!
BECAUSE YOU ARE!
OKAY, BILLY. WOULD YOU LIKE A HAIRCUT LIKE DR. BROWN'S?
NO THANKS, I WANT A HAIRCUT LIKE THIS!!!
ME

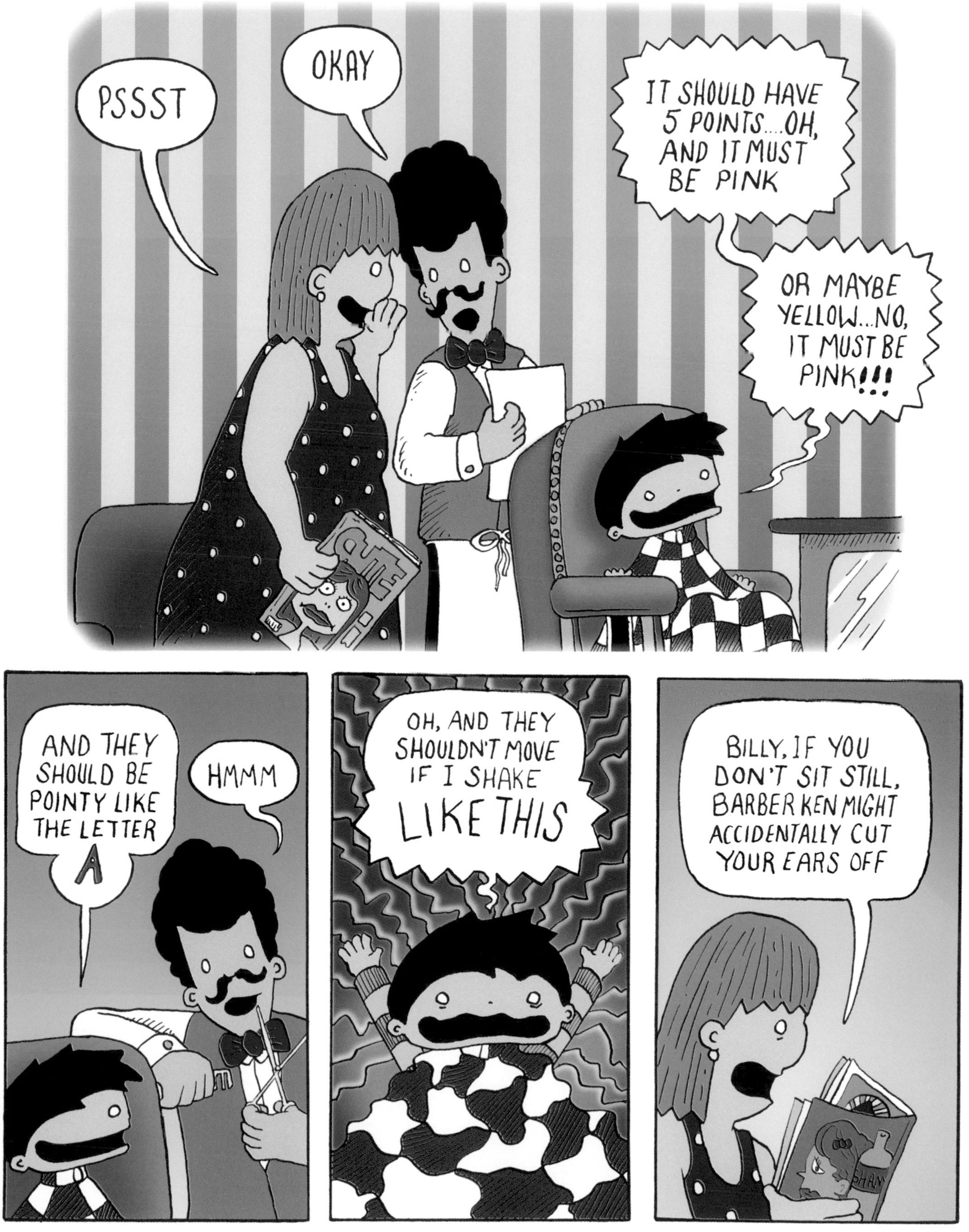
PSSST
OKAY
IT SHOULD HAVE 5 POINTS....OH, AND IT MUST BE PINK
OR MAYBE YELLOW...NO, IT MUST BE PINK!!!
AND THEY SHOULD BE POINTY LIKE THE LETTER A
HMMM
OH, AND THEY SHOULDN'T MOVE IF I SHAKE LIKE THIS
BILLY, IF YOU DON'T SIT STILL, BARBER KEN MIGHT ACCIDENTALLY CUT YOUR EARS OFF

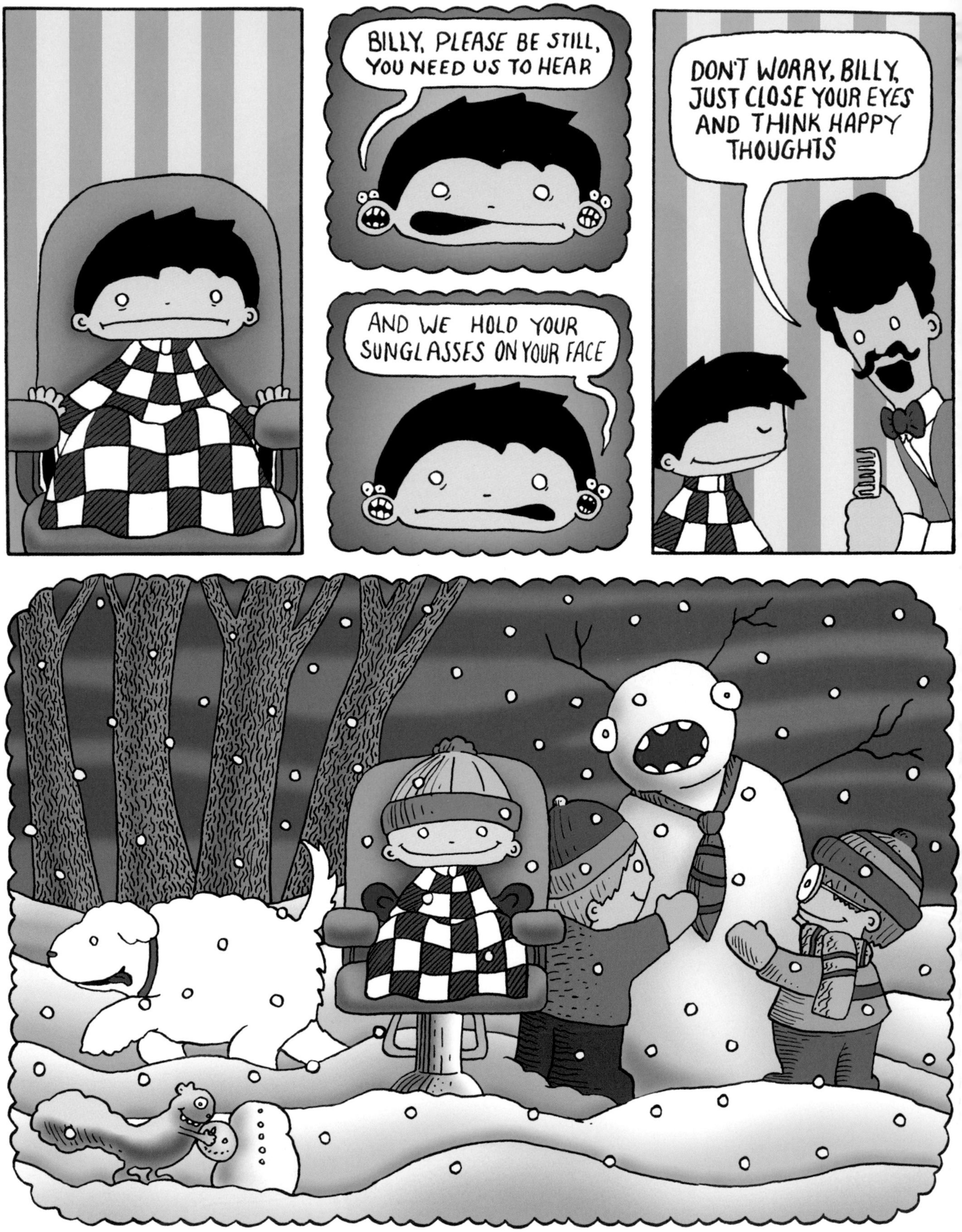
BILLY, PLEASE BE STILL, YOU NEED US TO HEAR
AND WE HOLD YOUR SUNGLASSES ON YOUR FACE
DON'T WORRY, BILLY, JUST CLOSE YOUR EYES AND THINK HAPPY THOUGHTS

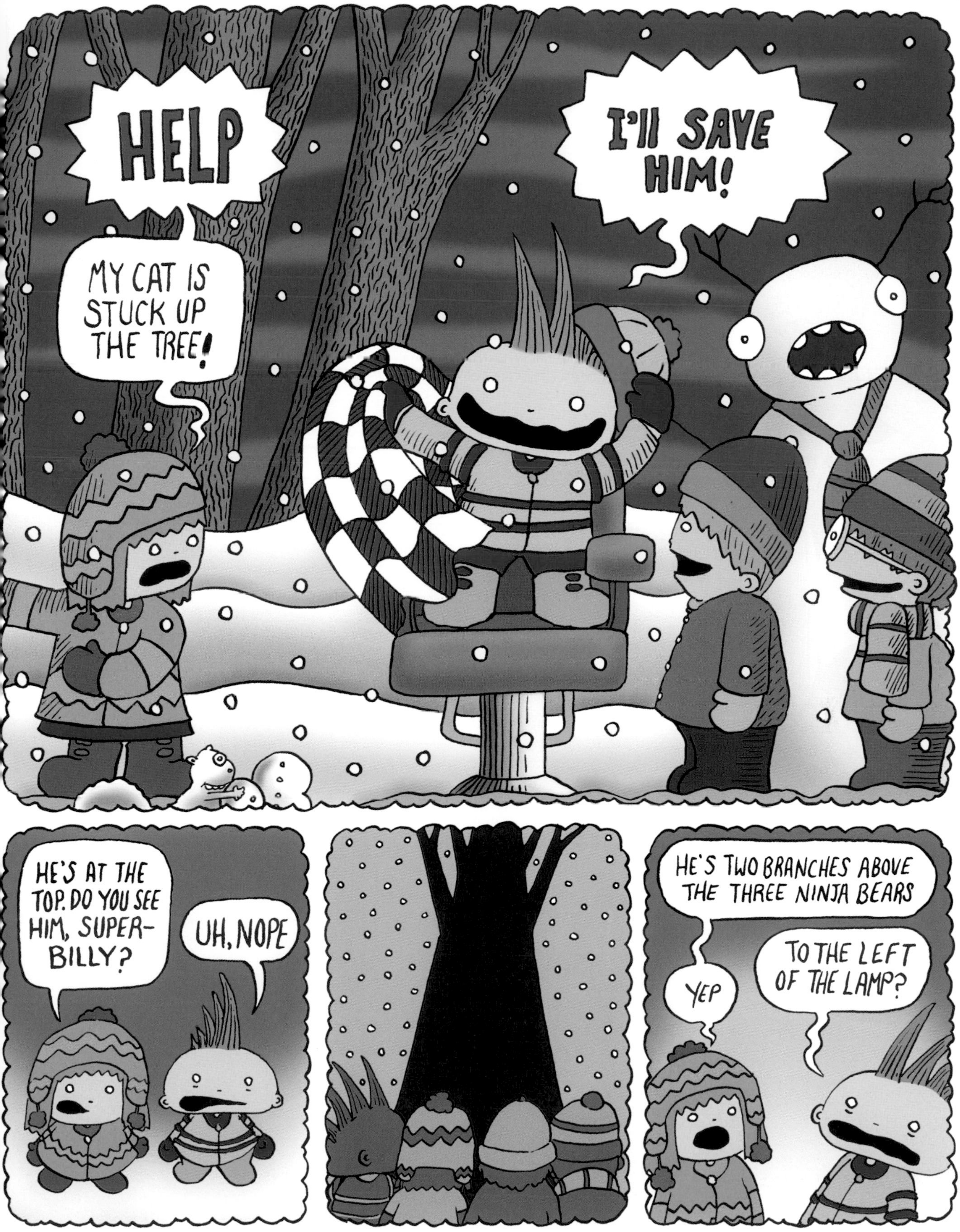
HELP
MY CAT IS STUCK UP THE TREE!
I'LL SAVE HIM!
HE'S AT THE TOP. DO YOU SEE HIM, SUPER-BILLY?
UH, NOPE
HE'S TWO BRANCHES ABOVE THE THREE NINJA BEARS
YEP
TO THE LEFT OF THE LAMP?

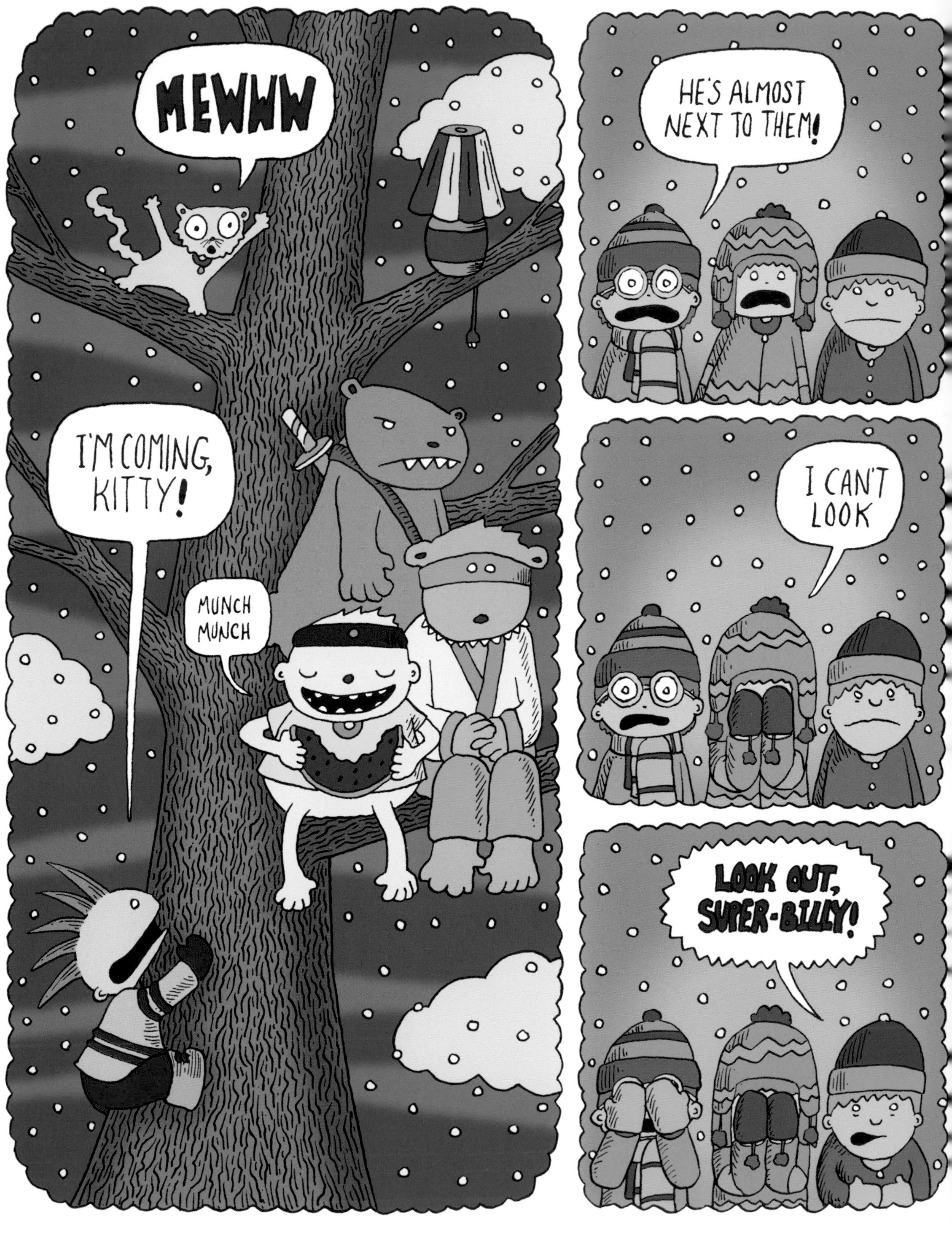
MEWWW
I'M COMING, KITTY!
MUNCH MUNCH
HE'S ALMOST NEXT TO THEM!
I CAN'T LOOK
LOOK OUT, SUPER-BILLY!

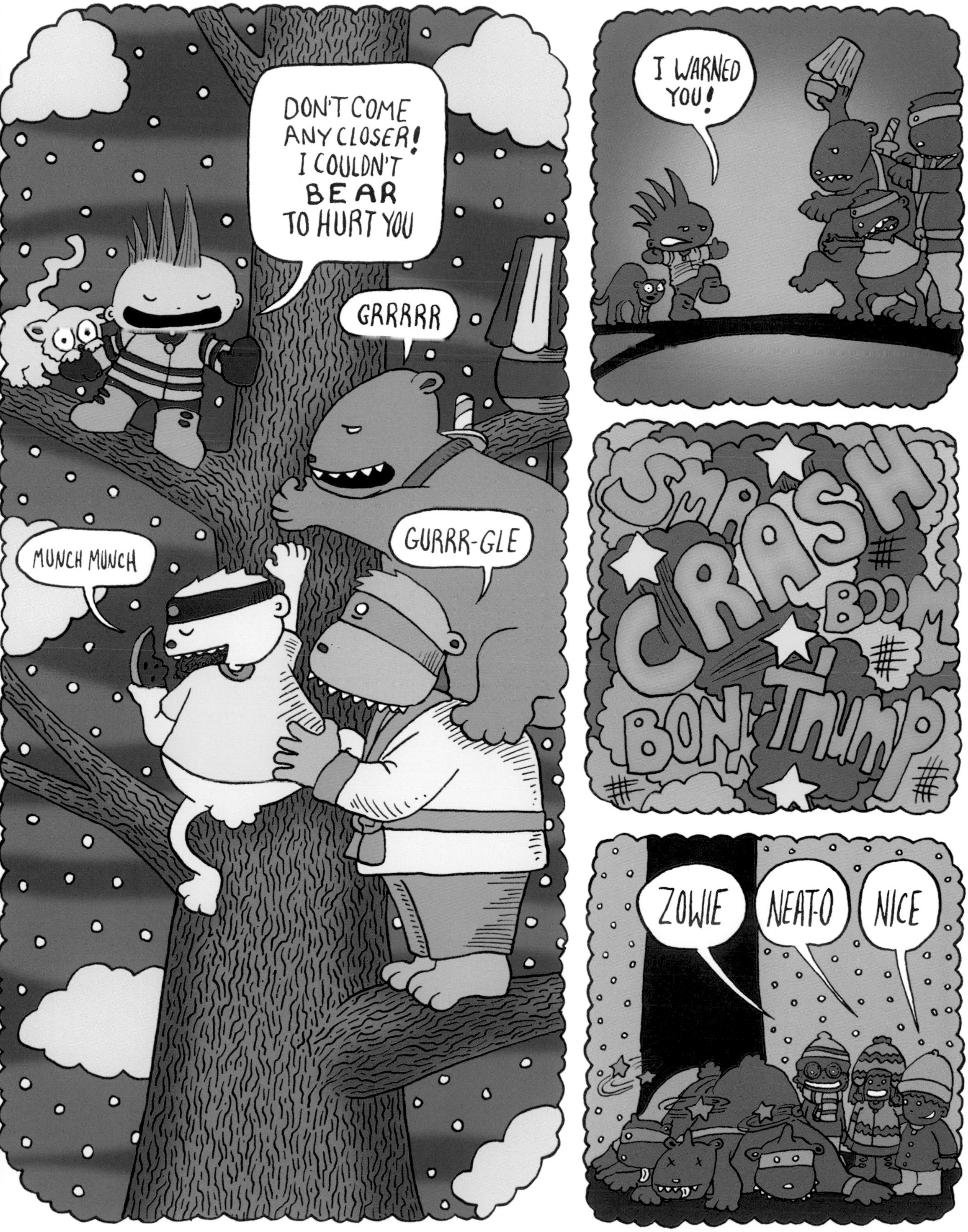
DON'T COME ANY CLOSER! I COULDN'T BEAR TO HURT YOU
GRRRRR
MUNCH MUNCH
GURRR-GLE
I WARNED YOU!
SMASH
CRASH
BOOM
BONK
THUMP
ZOWIE
NEAT-O
NICE

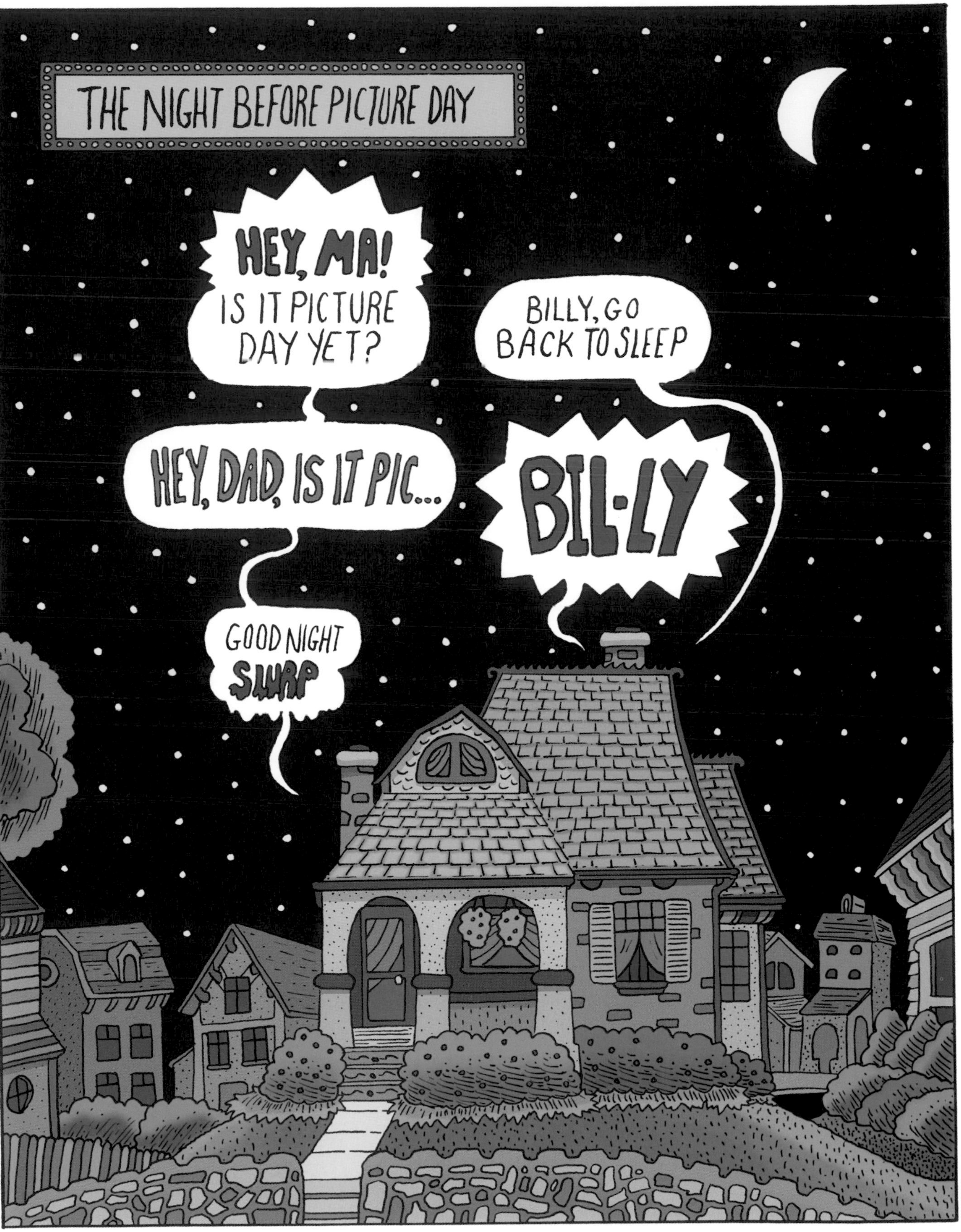

THE NIGHT BEFORE PICTURE DAY
HEY, MA! IS IT PICTURE DAY YET?
BILLY, GO BACK TO SLEEP
HEY, DAD, IS IT PIC...
BIL-LY
GOOD NIGHT SLURP

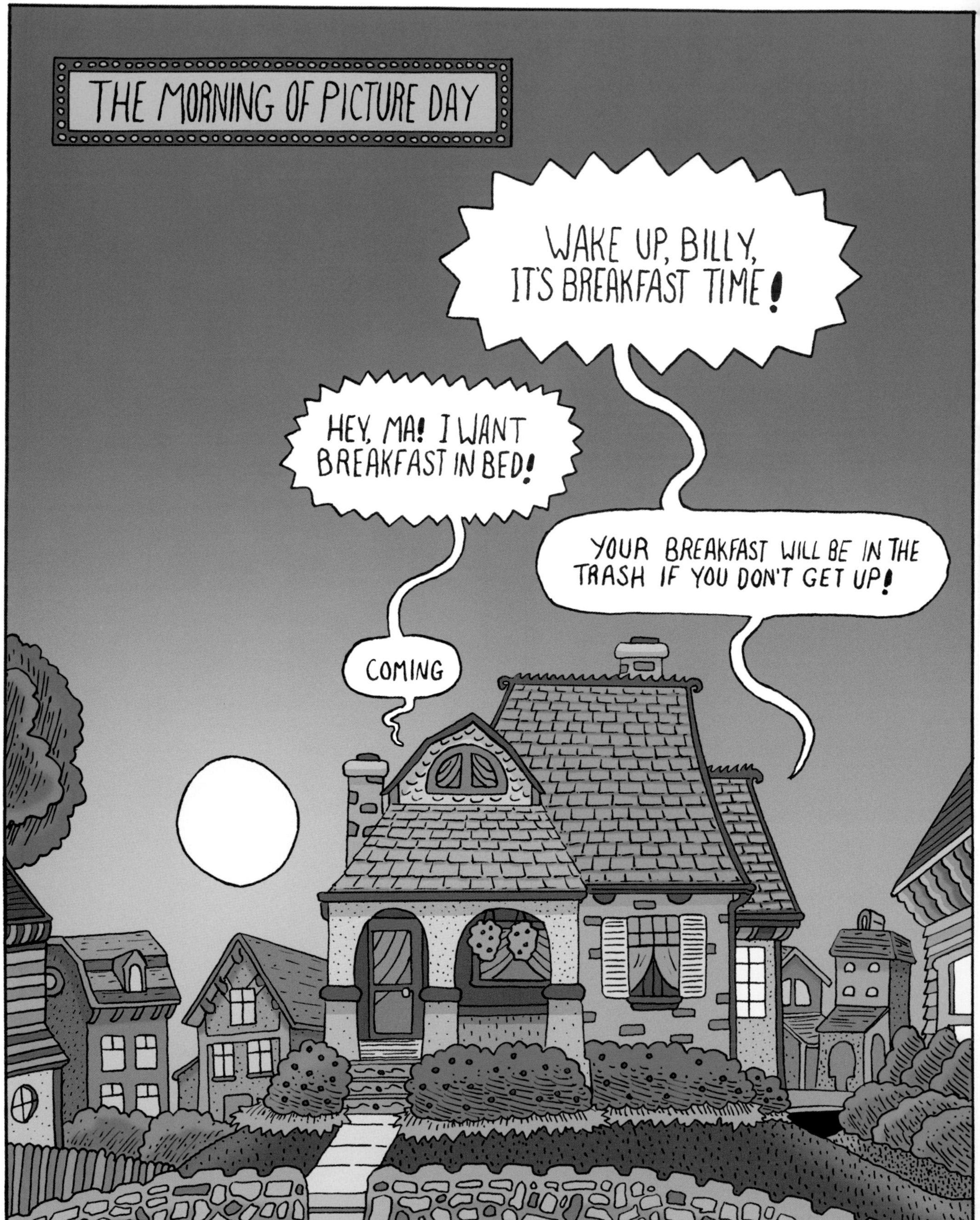
THE MORNING OF PICTURE DAY
WAKE UP, BILLY, IT'S BREAKFAST TIME!
HEY, MA! I WANT BREAKFAST IN BED!
YOUR BREAKFAST WILL BE IN THE TRASH IF YOU DON'T GET UP!
COMING

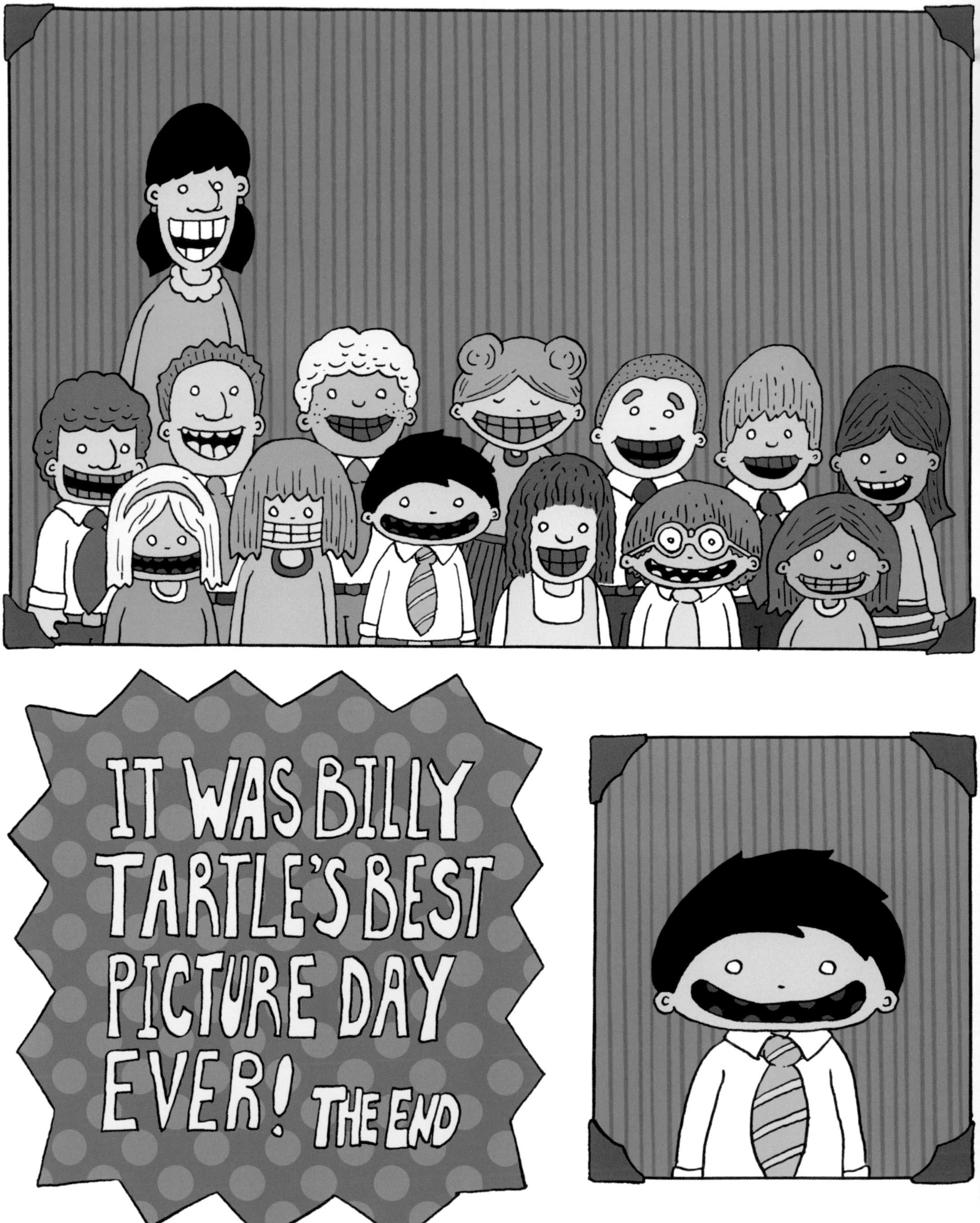
IT WAS BILLY TARTLE'S BEST PICTURE DAY EVER!
THE END

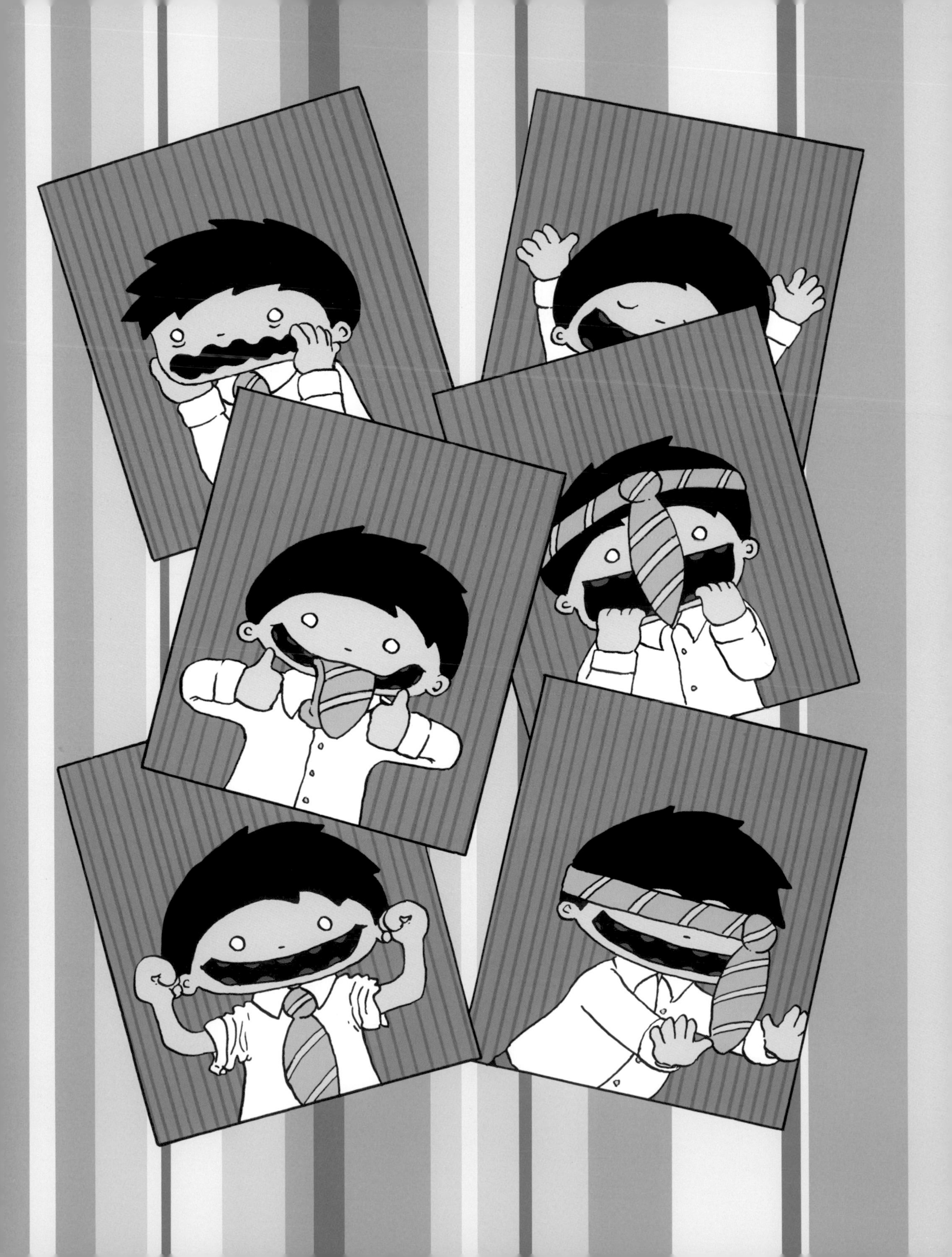

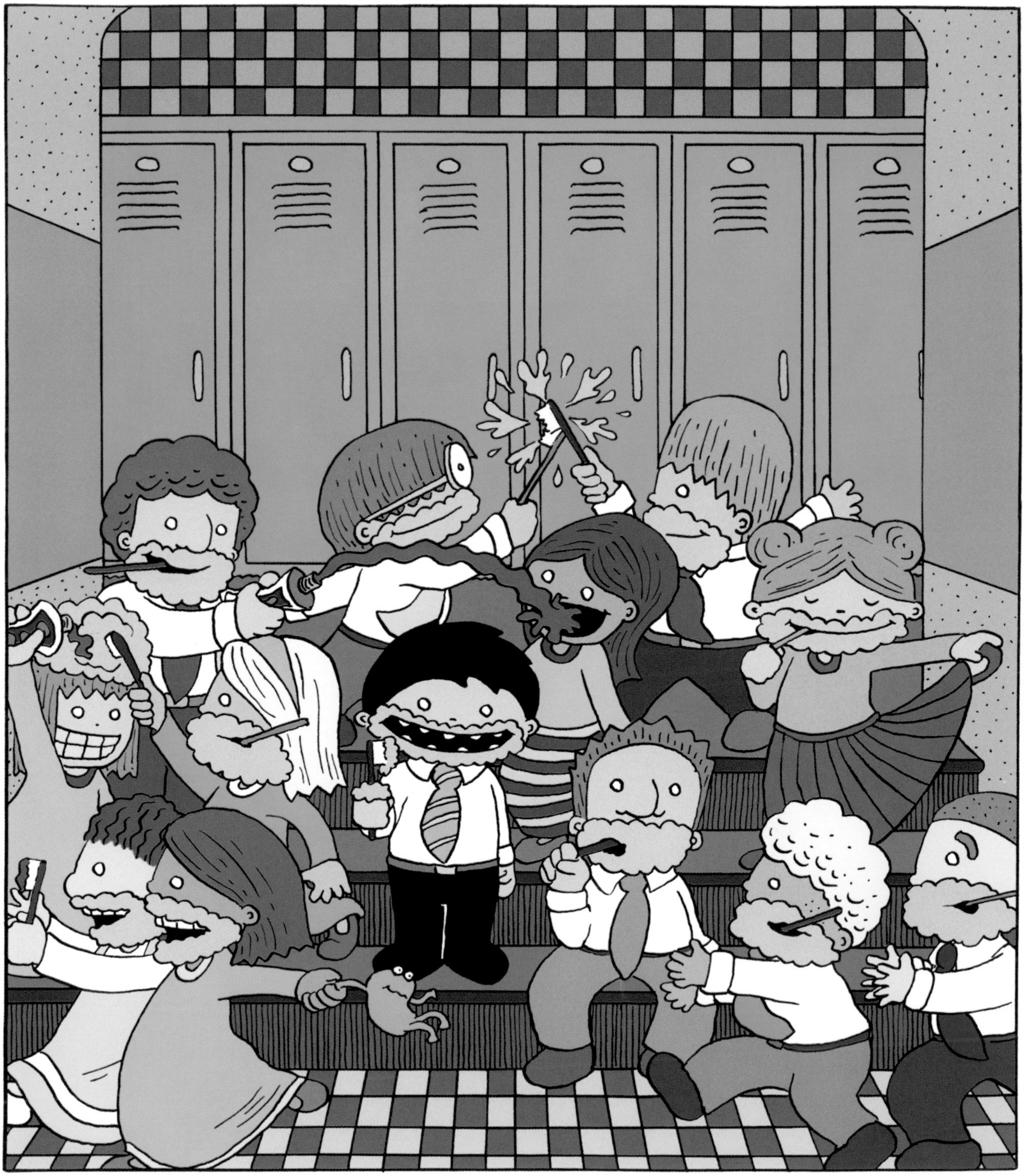

DATE DUE

OCT 0 5 2013

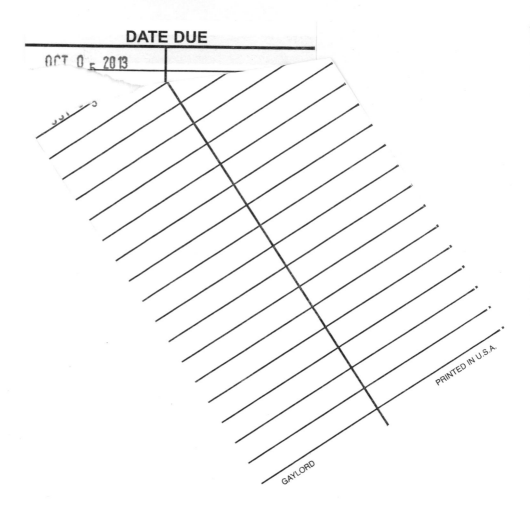

GAYLORD   PRINTED IN U.S.A.